# Dear Parent:
## Your child's love of reading starts here!

Every child learns to read in a different way and at his or her own speed. You can help your young reader improve and become more confident by encouraging his or her own interests and abilities. You can also guide your child's spiritual development by reading stories with biblical values and Bible stories, like I Can Read! books published by Zonderkidz. From books your child reads with you to the first books he or she reads alone, there are I Can Read! books for every stage of reading:

### SHARED READING
Basic language, word repetition, and whimsical illustrations, ideal for sharing with your emergent reader.

### BEGINNING READING
Short sentences, familiar words, and simple concepts for children eager to read on their own.

### READING WITH HELP
Engaging stories, longer sentences, and language play for developing readers.

### READING ALONE
Complex plots, challenging vocabulary, and high-interest topics for the independent reader.

### ADVANCED READING
Short paragraphs, chapters, and exciting themes for the perfect bridge to chapter books.

I Can Read! books have introduced children to the joy of reading since 1957. Featuring award-winning authors and illustrators and a fabulous cast of beloved characters, I Can Read! books set the standard for beginning readers.

A lifetime of discovery begins with the magical words "I Can Read!"

*Visit www.icanread.com for information on enriching your child's reading experience.*
*Visit www.zonderkidz.com for more Zonderkidz I Can Read! titles.*

"Be kind and compassionate
to one another."
*—Ephesians 4:32*

ZONDERKIDZ

*Princess Grace and Poppy*
Copyright © 2012 by Zonderkidz

Requests for information should be addressed to:

Zonderkidz, 5300 *Patterson Ave. SE, Grand Rapids, Michigan* 49530

Library of Congress Cataloging-in-Publication Data

Young, Jeanna Stolle, 1968–
    Princess Grace and Poppy / written by Jeanna Young & Jacqueline Johnson ;
illustrated by Omar Aranda.
        p. cm.
    ISBN 978-0-310-72677-7 (softcover)
    [1. Princesses—Fiction. 2. Christian life—Fiction. 3. Cats—Fiction. 4. Animals—Infancy—Fiction.
    5. Lost and found possessions—Fiction 6. Parables.] I. Johnson, Jacqueline Kinney, 1943–
    II. Aranda, Omar, ill. III. Title
    PZ7.Y8654Pn 2012
    [E]—dc23                                                                           2011043728

Editor: *Mary Hassinger*
Art direction & design: *Diane Mielke*

*Printed in China*

17 /DSC/ 10 9 8 7

I Can Read!™

The Princess Parables™

# Princess Grace and Poppy

Story inspired by **Jeanna Young** & **Jacqueline Johnson**
Pictures by **Omar Aranda**

Princess Grace lives in a castle.

She has four sisters.

They are Joy, Faith, Charity, and Hope.

Their daddy is the king!

One day, Grace dropped a vase.

While she was picking up

flowers, Grace heard a noise.

"Meow, meow, meow!"

Grace looked in the closet

under the stairs.

She said, "Five kittens!

How did you get in here?"

Joy, Faith, Charity,

and Hope went to see too.

Hope said, "It is five kittens!"

The king looked at the princesses.

The king looked at the kittens.

Grace said, "Daddy, I found

five kittens.

May we keep them, please?"

The king said, "We will talk about it."

Faith prayed, "Dear God, thank you for the kittens.

If daddy says yes, I promise to take care of them."

The king let the kittens
stay in the castle.

The princesses helped Grace with
one kitten each.

Princess Grace named her special
kitten Poppy.

Poppy was a happy kitten.

She loved to run and play.

Poppy even played at the

dinner table.

The princesses laughed.

But the king said,

"Grace, please stop Poppy."

Grace said, "Poppy! Please come

here."

Every day the princesses played

with the kittens.

Princess Charity said,

"My kitten has a green bow."

Princess Faith said,

"My kitten has a blue dress."

But Poppy was Grace's favorite
kitten of the litter.

She loved to play.

Poppy played hide-and-seek.

Grace called, "Where are you,
Poppy?"

Poppy ran from Grace.

She ran so fast! Boom!

Silly Poppy ran into the king's feet.

The king smiled.

"You are a special kitten, Poppy."

Then, one day, Princess Grace

could not find Poppy.

"One … two … three … four …

Poppy? Where are you?" Grace

cried out.

Her little kitten was not with

the others.

# Where could she be?

The king found Grace in the garden.

The princess was praying.

"Dear God, please take care

of little Poppy.

Keep her safe.

I love her very much."

The king said, "God hears

your prayers, Grace.

Ask him to keep Poppy safe.

And I will help you look for her."

Joy, Faith, Charity, Hope, and
Grace looked all over the castle.
Their father had said to look
everywhere.

So the princesses even looked in the
dark and scary Black Woods!
The princesses all called,
"Poppy, Poppy! Where are you?"

Grace was tired and worried.

She whispered a quiet prayer

for help.

Then Grace slipped and fell!

She fell in the grass by a log.

"Meow, meow," said a small voice.

Grace looked up.

She saw Poppy in the log.

Poppy was wet and messy,

but she was safe.

Grace wrapped Poppy in her cape.

The sisters rode back to the castle.

When the king saw the princesses

and Poppy, he was so happy.

The girls and Poppy were back home,
safe and sound.

"Welcome home!" the king shouted.

That night, the king and

princesses ate a treat.

The king said, "We are blessed.

We have each other.

And we have five kittens,

all safe and sound."

Grace looked at Poppy.

"Thank you, God," said Princess Grace.